KU-547-571

This *LADYBIRD TALE*
belongs to

....

Jack
and the
Beanstalk

Retold by Vera Southgate M.A., B.COM
with illustrations by Mélanie Florian

LADYBIRD 🐞 TALES

ONCE UPON A TIME there was a widow who had a lazy son called Jack. They lived together in a tiny cottage.

Jack and his mother were very poor. As time went on, they became poorer and poorer, while Jack grew lazier and lazier.

Soon Jack and his mother were so poor that all they had left in the world was one cow. At last the day arrived when Jack's mother said, "Tomorrow you must take our cow to market and sell her. She is all we have left in the world, so be sure that you get a good price for her."

The next day, Jack set off for market. On the road he met a butcher who asked him where he was going with the cow.

When Jack told him, the butcher said, "I will exchange these beans for your cow." He showed Jack some strange-looking beans, all of different colours.

"I would be a fool to exchange my cow for your beans," said Jack.

"Ah! But these are not ordinary beans," replied the butcher. "They are magic beans."

Jack thought what a fine thing it would be to have some magic beans, so he gave the cow to the butcher, put the beans in his pocket and set off for home.

"Look, Mother!" cried Jack. "I have exchanged our cow for these magic beans."

His mother was very, very angry. "You silly boy. Now we shall surely starve!"

In her anger, she threw the beans out of the window and sent Jack upstairs to bed without any supper.

The next morning, when Jack woke up, his room was much darker than usual. When he looked out of the window he saw that a huge beanstalk had sprung up during the night from the magic beans that his mother had thrown out of the window.

Jack ran outside and immediately began to climb the beanstalk. He climbed and climbed, but whenever he looked up, the top of the beanstalk still stretched upwards, out of sight.

After many hours of climbing, Jack reached the top of the beanstalk and stepped off into a wild, bare country. A long road led away into the distance.

Jack set off along the road and soon he met a very old woman.

"Good morning, Jack," she said. Jack was amazed that the woman knew his name.

"I know all about you," she said. "This land belongs to a wicked giant. When you were a baby, the giant stole all your father's belongings. That is why your mother is now so poor."

"You must try to get your father's wealth back," she continued. "If you are brave, I will try to help you."

At that the old woman disappeared, and Jack went forward along the lonely road.

Towards evening, Jack came to a castle. He knocked on the great door and a woman opened it.

"I am tired and hungry," said Jack. "Please can you give me some supper and a bed for the night?"

"Oh! My poor boy!" cried the woman. "My husband is a giant and he eats people. He would be sure to find you and eat you for his supper."

Jack felt afraid when he heard this, but he was too tired and hungry to go another step, so he pleaded with the woman to take him in.

At last the giant's wife agreed and she led Jack into her kitchen. Then she set a fine supper for him.

Scarcely had he finished eating when the ground was shaken by heavy, stamping feet. Three loud knocks were heard at the door. It was the giant returning home!

Jack's heart began to thump. The giant's wife began to shake. She grabbed Jack and pushed him into the oven, which fortunately was cold. Then she went to let her husband in.

The giant stomped into the kitchen, sniffed around and roared:

"Fee, fi, fo, fum,
I smell the blood
of an Englishman.
Be he alive or be he dead,
I'll grind his bones to make
my bread."

"Nonsense!" said the giant's wife. "You are dreaming," and she set an enormous meal on the table before him. As the giant was hungry, he sniffed no more but sat down to eat.

Jack peeped at the giant through a crack in the oven door. He was astonished to see how much the giant ate.

When the giant had finished his meal, he shouted to his wife, "Bring me my hen!" His wife brought the hen and went off to bed.

"Lay!" shouted the giant, whereupon the hen laid a golden egg.

"Another!" roared the giant, and the hen laid another.

Again and again, in a voice of thunder, the giant shouted, "Lay!"

Soon there were twelve golden eggs on the table. Then the giant fell asleep in his chair and he snored so loudly that the castle shook.

As soon as Jack heard the snores of the giant, he crept out of the oven, seized the hen and tiptoed out of the castle.

Then he set off running along the road, as fast as ever he could. On and on he ran, until at last he came to the top of the beanstalk. He climbed down quickly and took the wonderful hen to his poor mother.

When Jack set the hen on the table and ordered it to lay a golden egg, Jack's mother could not believe her eyes. "Now our worries are over," she said.

But, after a while, Jack longed for another adventure. He was determined to visit the giant's castle again. He disguised himself so that the giant's wife would not know him.

Just as before, Jack climbed the beanstalk and reached the castle towards evening. When the giant's wife opened the door, he said, "I'm hungry and tired. Can I stay for the night?"

"You cannot stay here," replied the giant's wife. "The last boy I took in stole my husband's hen."

But Jack chatted so pleasantly that eventually the giant's wife let him in.

After Jack had eaten a good
supper, the giant's wife hid him in
a cupboard. No sooner had she
done this when in stomped the
giant, roaring:

> *"Fee, fi, fo, fum,*
> *I smell the blood*
> *of an Englishman.*
> *Be he alive or be he dead,*
> *I'll grind his bones to make*
> *my bread."*

"Nonsense!" said the giant's wife.
"You are dreaming," and she set an
enormous supper before him.

After supper the giant roared,
"Fetch me my money bags."
His wife brought the bags and
went off to bed.

The giant emptied all the money
onto the table, and counted it
over and over again before putting
it back into the bags. Then he
fell asleep.

As soon as Jack heard the giant's
snores, he crept out of the cupboard
and picked up the heavy money
bags. He managed to sling them
over his shoulder, then he let
himself out of the castle as quietly
as possible.

Jack could not run along the road because the money bags were so heavy, but he reached the top of the beanstalk safely.

Jack's mother was overjoyed to see him, and when he emptied the money bags on the table, she was astonished.

With the money, they built a bigger house and bought furniture, new clothes and food.

Jack and his mother were very contented. But soon Jack began to long for more adventure. He was determined to visit the giant's castle once more.

This time, Jack used a different disguise.

Once again, Jack climbed the beanstalk, followed the same path and arrived at the castle door. The giant's wife did not recognize him and he begged for a night's lodging.

"No, no!" she cried. "You cannot come in here. The last two boys that I took in were thieves. No, no, you cannot come in."

Jack begged and begged and at last the giant's wife took pity on him, let him in and gave him some supper. Then she hid him in the wash-basket in the corner.

Soon the giant came home, and roared:

"Fee, fi, fo, fum,
I smell the blood
of an Englishman.
Be he alive, or be he dead,
I'll grind his bones to make
my bread."

"Nonsense!" said the giant's wife. "You are dreaming," and she set an enormous supper before him.

After supper the giant shouted, "Bring me my harp!" The giant's wife brought a beautiful golden harp and set it on the table before him. Then she went off to bed.

"Play!" roared the giant, and the harp began to play of its own accord. Jack had never heard such sweet music. The harp continued to play until the giant was almost asleep. Then he shouted "Stop!" and the music stopped.

As soon as Jack heard the loud snores of the giant, he jumped out of the corner and seized the harp. But the harp called out, "Master, master!"

The giant woke up in a fury. "You are the boy who stole my hen and my money bags," he bellowed. Then he staggered to his feet and set off after Jack.

Jack was terrified. He ran for his life towards the beanstalk. Looking over his shoulder, Jack saw the giant striding after him. Then he ran as fast as he had ever run before in his life.

Jack reached the top of the beanstalk safely, but the giant was close behind him. He scrambled and slid down the beanstalk, shouting, "Mother, Mother, bring me the axe quickly. The giant is coming."

Then Jack's mother brought her son the axe. By then the giant was climbing rapidly down the beanstalk.

Jack swung the axe with all his strength, and gave one mighty blow at the beanstalk.

The beanstalk toppled down and there was a tremendous thud as the giant was thrown headlong to the ground. The giant fell dead in Jack's garden and so big was he that he filled it from end to end.

Pointing at the giant, Jack said to his mother, "He robbed us of all our wealth."

At that moment, there appeared the old woman who had talked to Jack.

She told them that she was really
a fairy and that it was she who
had made Jack take the magic
beans in exchange for the cow.
She had wanted him to climb the
beanstalk, and she had led him to
the giant's castle.

"Your troubles are now over,"
the fairy told Jack and his mother.
"You will never be poor again and
you will be happy as long as
you live."

And so it was. Jack and his mother
lived happily ever after.

A History of Jack and the Beanstalk

The story of *Jack and the Beanstalk* might be an old English fairy tale but this tale has inspired pantomimes, films and even computer games!

English publisher and bookseller Benjamin Tabart published the earliest written version of the story in 1807.

Since then, there have many versions of the tale, but Joseph Jacobs' retelling, published in 1890 and based on the versions he heard as a child, is the most popular today.

The most famous line of the story is the giant's poem: *"Fee, fi, fo, fum, I smell the blood of an Englishman..."*, and children love to read this aloud.

Vera Southgate's 1965 classic Ladybird version has delighted thousands of children, reinforcing its popularity.

Collect more fantastic

LADYBIRD 🐞 TALES

9781409311072

9781409311119

9781409311102

9781409311126

The
Gingerbread
Man

9781409311096

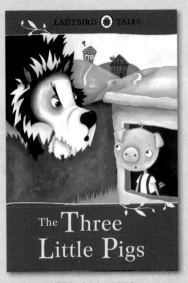

The Three
Little Pigs

9781409311089

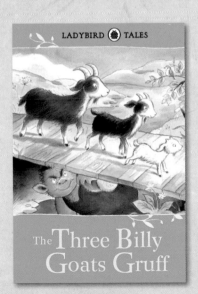

The Three Billy
Goats Gruff

9781409311065

Hansel
and Gretel

9781409311133

Endpapers taken from series 606d,
first published in 1964

A catalogue record for this book is available from the British Library
Published by Ladybird Books Ltd
80 Strand London WC2R 0RL
A Penguin Company

005

ISBN: 978-1-40931-110-2

Printed in China